Bruce Wayne

...ination Award recipient and distinguished gentleman

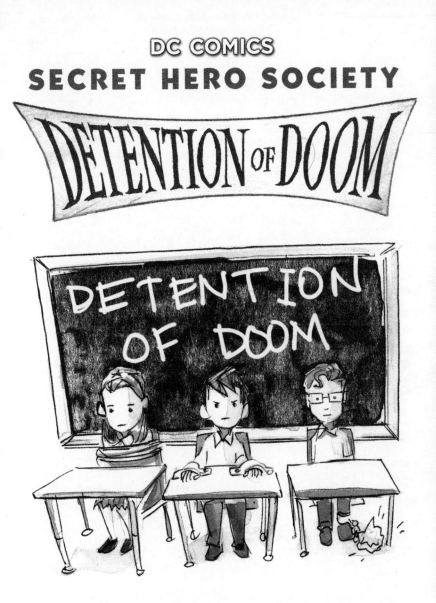

DC COMICS
SECRET HERO SOCIETY

DETENTION OF DOOM

DETENTION OF DOOM

Written by **Derek Fridolfs** | Illustrations by **Dustin Nguyen**

SCHOLASTIC

To all my wonderful teachers and educators throughout the years at McCardle Elementary, Ahwahnee Middle School, and Hoover High School, allowing for my mind to wander, be inspired, and get creative. And still I managed to stay out of detention!

— Derek

Thank you to my wife, Nicole, for the love, support, and taking care of real-life things so that I can live in the imaginary. My kids, Bradley and Kaeli, for keeping me always inspired and forever excited about the things to come.

— Dustin

SCHOLASTIC CHILDREN'S BOOKS
EUSTON HOUSE,
24 EVERSHOLT STREET,
LONDON NW1 1DB, UK

A DIVISION OF SCHOLASTIC LTD
LONDON ~ NEW YORK ~ TORONTO ~ SYDNEY ~ AUCKLAND
MEXICO CITY ~ NEW DELHI ~ HONG KONG

FIRST PUBLISHED IN THE US BY SCHOLASTIC INC, 2018
THIS EDITION PUBLISHED IN THE UK BY SCHOLASTIC LTD, 2018

BOOK DESIGN BY RICK DEMONICO AND CHEUNG TAI

ISBN 978 1407 18420 3

A CIP CATALOGUE RECORD FOR THIS BOOK
IS AVAILABLE FROM THE BRITISH LIBRARY.

PRINTED IN THE UK BY CPI GROUP (UK) LTD, CROYDON, CRO 4YY
PAPERS USED BY SCHOLASTIC CHILDREN'S BOOKS
ARE MADE FROM WOOD GROWN IN SUSTAINABLE FORESTS

10 9 8 7 6 5 4 3 2 1

WWW.SCHOLASTIC.CO.UK

CITY OF GOTHAM

Dear Bruce Wayne,

Join us as we recognize outstanding students gathered across every school district for their academic achievements and community outreach. Awards will be presented at approximately twelve noon at Gotham City Hall, followed by refreshments in the foyer.

We hope to see you there!

Office of the Mayor

COMPUTER SCIENCE -------- VICTOR STONE

PLANT SCIENCE ------------ PAMELA ISLEY

DEBATE -------------------- GUY GARDNER

JOURNALISM -------------- LOIS LANE

MARKSMANSHIP ----------- FLOYD LAWTON

MUSICAL ACHIEVEMENT ---- DINAH LANCE

CONGRATULATIONS ON YOUR OUTSTANDING ACADEMICS!

AWARDS SPONSORED BY THE LUTHOR FOUNDATION

9

GROUP CHAT

yeah man

I think it's some sort of group in Metropolis

do ya want me to beef up your credentials so you can have access?

nope I'll just sneak in

don't get caught ;)

ya know ya might wanna just call Lex

well sure but

I've forwarded you his number and the one for Luthor Tower

< USER HAS LOGGED OFF >

SEND

18

21

23

it's found something related to space debris that LuthorCorp is involved in

something they acquired in Smallville

it's not much but it's a start

thanks

no prob

here to help

USERNAME: BWAYNE
RE: JOURNAL ENTRY 1

CLARK REMAINS MISSING, NO DOUBT THANKS TO LEX. THAT KID HAS HAD IT IN FOR CLARK EVER SINCE THEY RAN AGAINST EACH OTHER FOR SCHOOL PRESIDENT. ONE MINUTE, CLARK IS AT MY HOME CHECKING OUT HIS TROPHY. THE NEXT MINUTE, THE TROPHY MADE HIM DISAPPEAR! IT MAKES ME HATE TROPHIES EVEN MORE NOW.

SOME FRIENDS AND I WENT TO TRACK DOWN LEX TO GET TO THE BOTTOM OF IT, BUT LEX WAS NO HELP. HE'S NOT VERY GOOD AT PLAYING COY, AS I CAN TELL. HE WAS JUST LYING WHENEVER WE ASKED HIM FOR HIS HELP. LUTHORCORP WAS RESPONSIBLE FOR OFFERING THE SCHOOL TROPHIES, BUT WE'VE COME UP EMPTY FINDING OUT WHY OR HOW THEY'RE INVOLVED.

BUT NOW VIC HAS OFFERED SOME INFORMATION PERTAINING TO LUTHORCORP IN SMALLVILLE, WHICH IS CLARK'S HOMETOWN. IT'S WORTH CHECKING INTO. IT'S LUCKY I STILL HAVE ACCESS TO MY ALLOWANCE, BECAUSE I'M GOING TO NEED IT TO ORDER SOME BUS TICKETS ONLINE FOR DIANA AND ME TO GO CHECK THINGS OUT. BARRY'S ON HIS OWN. THAT KID CAN RUN THERE! BESIDES, I WON'T HAVE TO HEAR HIM CONSTANTLY TALKING AND BEING ANNOYING.

it's taking you guys forever

are you already there Barry?

yeah like hours ago

buses are for losers

I've already run across Smallville and checked the whole town out

lots of farms and cows

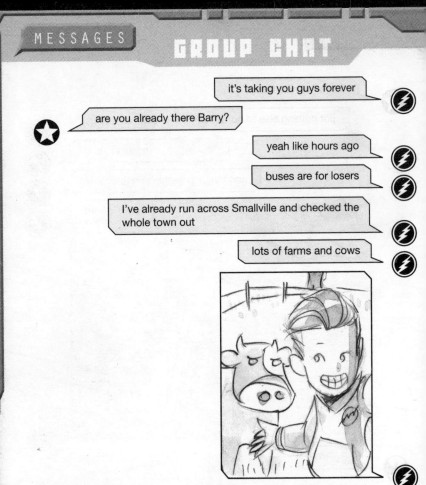

moooooooo

Barry!

why would Clark want to live here?

Smallville

more like Dullsville

SEND

FROM: PENNY_1
TO: BWAYNE
SUBJECT: WHERE ARE YOU?

MASTER BRUCE,

WHEN YOU INVITE FRIENDS OVER FOR LUNCH, IT IS
RESPONSIBLE OF THE HOST TO ACTUALLY REMAIN FOR IT.
YOU DIDN'T EVEN LEAVE A FORWARDING NOTE REGARDING
WHERE YOU AND YOUR FRIENDS TOOK OFF TO.

SINCE YOU ARE NOT ANSWERING YOUR TEXTS, I HOPE YOU
RECEIVE THIS EMAIL AND CALL TO LET ME KNOW YOUR
LOCATION. I REGRET TO INFORM YOU THAT YOUR LUNCH IS
NOW COLD AND EATEN. DON'T LET YOUR DINNER SUFFER THE
SAME FATE.

SINCERELY,

ALFRED

Smallville Gazette

THE SKY IS FALLING
Asteroids Descend on Smallville

Local farmers put their crops and families to bed overnight, only to wake up the next morning to an invasion. "I heard the sound of something hitting the barn. And when I checked the fields, there were craters," said Theodore MacDonald. "It's like nothing I ever seen!"

All reports and eyewitness accounts seem to point to a meteor shower that rained down over Smallville, leaving miles of rocky debris along roads and fields. The damage is still being calculated.

"Meteors falling through our atmosphere is very common," said a spokesperson from S.T.A.R. Labs, located in Metropolis. "But most disintegrate upon entry into Earth's atmosphere. It's rare for so many meteorites to remain intact."

Story continued on page A7

S.T.A.R. LABS

31

FROM: BWAYNE
TO: V-BORG
SUBJECT: CHECK THIS OUT!

VIC,

I'VE ATTACHED SOME FILES OF THINGS I'VE FOUND RELATED
TO LUTHORCORP'S INVOLVEMENT IN SMALLVILLE. THEY WERE
CLOSE TO THE KENT FARM WHEN THIS HAPPENED MANY YEARS
AGO. LOOK INTO THIS FURTHER IF YOU CAN. THE SMALLVILLE
GAZETTE ARTICLE IS VERY INTERESTING.

—B

33

35

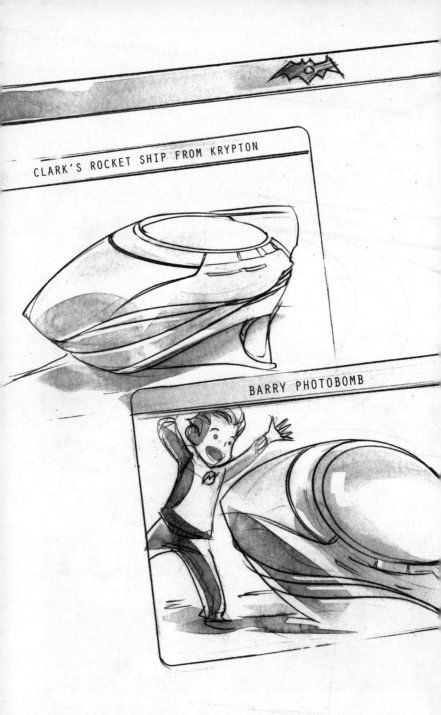

CLARK'S ROCKET SHIP FROM KRYPTON

BARRY PHOTOBOMB

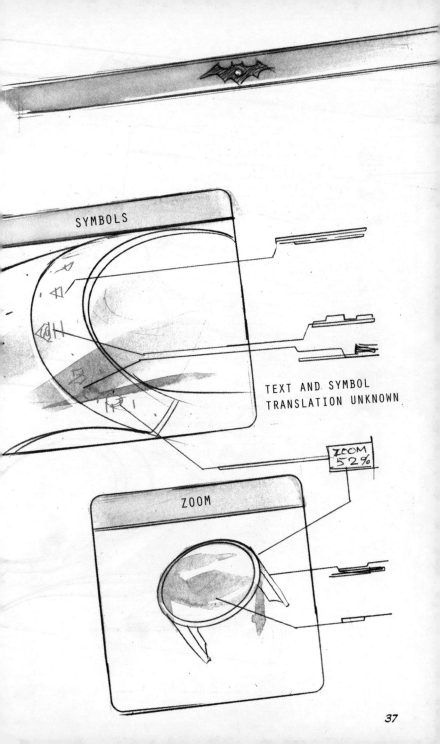

SYMBOLS

TEXT AND SYMBOL
TRANSLATION UNKNOWN

ZOOM
52%

ZOOM

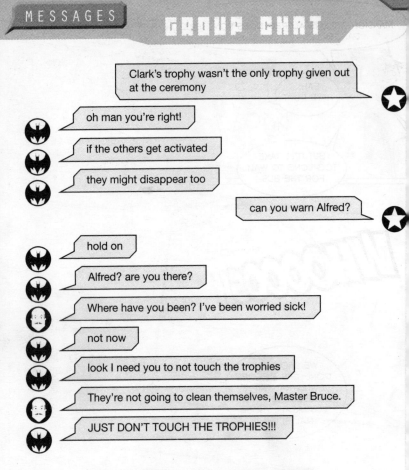

Clark's trophy wasn't the only trophy given out at the ceremony

oh man you're right!

if the others get activated

they might disappear too

can you warn Alfred?

hold on

Alfred? are you there?

Where have you been? I've been worried sick!

not now

look I need you to not touch the trophies

They're not going to clean themselves, Master Bruce.

JUST DON'T TOUCH THE TROPHIES!!!

< USER HAS LOGGED OFF >

SEND

43

DIAGNOSTIC CHECK

SIZE
DIMENSIONS: 60.96CM X
20.32CM X 12.70CM

COMPOSITION: FOREIGN
ALLOY—UNDETERMINED

DIAGNOSTIC
ESTIMATED TIME
UNTIL COMPLETION

CALCULATING . .
4 HOURS
25 MINUTES . .

47

DETENTION REPORT #1:

RUNNING THROUGH THE HALLS

DETENTION REPORT #2:

TALKING IN CLASS

DETENTION REPORT #3:

CAFETERIA FOOD FIGHT

DETENTION REPORT #4:

ACCESSING TEACHERS' LOUNGE

DETENTION REPORT #5:

STACKING DESKS

DETENTION
REPORT #6:

STEALING TARDY
SLIPS

DETENTION
REPORT #7:

WATER
FOUNTAIN
PRANK

DETENTION
REPORT #8:

SCHOOL FLAGPOLE
PRANK

DETENTION
REPORT #9:

THE RUBBER DUCK
INCIDENT

DETENTION
REPORT #10:

REARRANGING
PRINCIPAL'S
OFFICE

50

ROBOTIC DRONE!

HOMING BEACON:
DETACHABLE AND
TRACKABLE

WINGS:
ROTOR BLADES
ALLOW FOR
HOVERING

SPEAKER:
VOICE-ACTIVATED

COMPUTER DEVICE:
CAN RECORD
JOURNAL ENTRIES TO
BATCOMPUTER

DIGITAL CAMERA LENS:
CAPTURES VISUALS IN
HI-DEF

USERNAME: BWAYNE
RE: JOURNAL ENTRY 2

WE'VE FOUND OURSELVES TRANSPORTED INTO THIS PHANTOM
DETENTION. IT'S PRESUMABLY THE SAME PLACE CLARK
DISAPPEARED INTO, ALTHOUGH WE HAVEN'T SEEN HIM.

THIS PLACE IS PRETTY BARREN. IT'S LIKE A BEACH WITHOUT
THE FUN, OR SO I'M TOLD BY BARRY AND HIS NEED FOR HUMOR
TO LIGHTEN THE MOOD.

LUCKILY MY ROBOTIC DRONE AND BATCOMPUTER WERE SUCKED
INSIDE WITH THE REST OF US. THEY'RE ALLOWING ME TO
RECORD THESE JOURNALS AS WELL AS PROVIDE OTHER HELPFUL
TOOLS AS WE NAVIGATE HERE.

ANOTHER THING ODD ABOUT THIS PLACE IS NO ONE CAN USE
THEIR POWERS. BARRY CAN'T MOVE SUPER-FAST, EVEN IF HE'S
ANNOYING AT ANY SPEED. DIANA'S STRENGTH IS GONE. VIC'S
CYBERNETIC PARTS ARE UNRELIABLE AND FALLING APART. AND
OLIVER'S TARGETING SKILLS ARE OFF, ALTHOUGH IT MIGHT BE
DUE TO THE GRAVIMETRIC PROPERTIES OF THIS DIMENSION.

STILL . . . I HOPE WE CAN FIND CLARK AND GET OUT OF
HERE. I MISS MY CAVE.

My name is Clark Kent and I'm lost. I have no idea where I am or how I got here. But I've been trying to find a way out. I've walked in many directions, but this place is playing tricks with my eyes. I think I'm just walking in a circle.

I hope someone reads this who can help me out. Maybe even my friends. Thanks!

CLARK IS HERE! WE HAVEN'T SEEN HIM YET BUT WE FOUND A
NOTE THAT HE LEFT BEHIND FOR US. IT MAKES ME WONDER HOW
MANY OTHER PEOPLE MIGHT BE STUCK HERE, TOO.

IT'S IMPOSSIBLE TO TRACK ANYONE IN THIS SAND. OR
IT COULD BE THAT WE HAVEN'T BEEN ABLE TO FIND ANY
FOOTPRINTS. BUT IF CLARK KEEPS LEAVING NOTES, THEN MAYBE
THEY'LL LEAD US RIGHT TO HIM.

I HOPE WE CAN FIND HIM QUICKLY. THERE'S A REASON WHY
PEOPLE STAY OUT OF THE DESERT. IT'S UNBEARABLY HOT,
UNCOMFORTABLE, AND WALKING ACROSS THE SHIFTING SAND CAN
MAKE ONE FEEL NAUSEOUS. THIS DETENTION HAS THE EFFECT
THAT I MISS SCHOOL, OR AT LEAST ALFRED. IF HE WERE HERE,
HE'D BE ABLE TO BRING ME SOMETHING COLD TO DRINK.

This is Clark again. I think I'm not the only one stuck here. I think others are trapped here as well. Sometimes I notice shapes moving in the distance that look like people. There's also weird messages scribbled on rocks.

I'm going to try to find anyone else who's here. Maybe together we can find a way out.

DRONE FOOTAGE

61

USERNAME: BWAYNE
RE: JOURNAL ENTRY 4

WE FOUND CLARK . . . KIND OF. OKAY, NOT REALLY.

THIS KID LOOKS A LITTLE LIKE CLARK . . . IF HE HAD
FALLEN OFF HIS TRACTOR BACK ON THE FARM. AND THEN THE
TRACTOR DROVE OVER HIM. MULTIPLE TIMES. OVER AND OVER.

HIS NAME IS BIZARRO AND HE SPEAKS FUNNY. ALMOST SAYING
WORDS THAT HAVE THE OPPOSITE MEANING. MAKING IT TOUGH TO
UNDERSTAND WHAT HE'S SAYING AT TIMES. IT MAKES ME WONDER
HOW HE GOT HERE.

HE SEEMS HARMLESS ENOUGH. AND HE'S JOINED US, FOLLOWING
ALONG LIKE A PUPPY DOG, AS WE CONTINUE TO LOOK FOR
CLARK.

Comparison Chart

Clark

Bizarro

Shy

S

Speaks in full
Sentences

Not Shy

Backward
S

Speaks
backward

ME AM LEARN YOU HOW SPEAK AM ME AM USE FIVE HARD STEPS

1) ME AM ME ← (me = you)

2) YOU AM YOU ← (you = me)

3) THEY AM THEY ← (they = they)

NOW YOU AM BIZARRO LIKE ME AM ←
(Now you are Bizarro like I am)

BOOoo AND CLAP LEGS
(Cheer and clap hands)

YOU AM FAIL BECOME BIZARRO
(You have become Bizarro)

I still can't find a way out or anyone else. And my head feels a little woozy. I can't tell up from down in this place.

I don't even have ~~powers~~ I mean, I don't have the power to do anything in here. I hope my friends find me. But if they do, they'll probably be stuck, too. So maybe it's for the best if they don't find me.

This is my last note. If you find this, go back. You'll better off than me.

DETENTION DANGERS

NO DIVING OFF CLIFFS!

WATCH YOUR STEP! CANYONS!

NO GOLFING HERE— SANDPITS!

BEWARE YOUR SHADOW . . . ANY SHADOWS

73

HOMING BEACON INACCESSIBLE
DAMAGE TO TARGETING UNIT
FUNCTIONALITY 0%
SYSTEM REPAIR NEEDED

75

USERNAME: BWAYNE
RE: JOURNAL ENTRY 5

WE WERE ABLE TO FIND CLARK! DIANA TELLS ME IT WAS CLARK WHO FOUND US. I DON'T CARE. I'M JUST HAPPY HE'S OKAY.

THIS DETENTION REALLY HAS PHANTOMS AFTER ALL! THEY COME OUT OF THE SHADOWS AND ARE LIKE GHOSTS. WE'RE UNABLE TO FIGHT THEM, BECAUSE IF WE GET TOUCHED, THEY CAN STEAL OUR SPIRIT . . . AT LEAST THAT'S WHAT CLARK BELIEVES. THE ONLY THING THAT SCARED THEM AWAY WAS CREATING A TORCH FOR LIGHT. I JUST WISH CLARK HADN'T DESTROYED MY BAT COSTUME IN THE PROCESS. IT'S THE ONLY ONE I BROUGHT WITH ME.

AND MORE BAD NEWS IS, THE DRONE WAS DAMAGED DURING THE FIGHT. ITS HOMING BEACON DOESN'T WORK. IF WE CAN'T REPAIR IT, WE WON'T BE ABLE TO FIND OUR WAY BACK.

CLARK SAYS THERE ARE OTHERS HERE WHO ARE STUCK IN DETENTION. HE WANTS US TO RESCUE THEM, TOO. IT LOOKS LIKE WE'VE GOT OUR WORK CUT OUT FOR US!

BARRY'S DETENTION GUIDE:
GETTING TO KNOW YOUR DETENTIONS

DETENTION

report to homeroom
for detention

sit at desk and wait
for bell to leave

get yelled at by
teachers

no passing notes

sit at desk with nothing
to do

find friends in
detention

avoid spitballs

PHANTOM DETENTION

get sucked inside scary
dimention

sit in sand and never leave

get chased by Phantoms

no use of powers

walk in desert and be lost

find friends in phantom
detention

avoid sandstorms

81

SO THE PHANTOM DETENTION WAS CREATED, AS A ZONE TO HOLD BAD STUDENTS SO THEY MIGHT REFLECT ON THEIR ACTIONS.

THE HOUSE OF EL WAS RESPONSIBLE FOR BUILDING THE PHANTOM PROJECTOR TO SEND BAD STUDENTS THERE.

BEWARE THE PHANTOM DETENTION! IT CAN PLAY TRICKS ON YOUR MIND OR CREATE BACKWARD DUPLICATES TO FOOL YOU. THOSE UNWILLING TO LEARN FROM THEIR MISTAKES ARE DOOMED TO BECOME PHANTOMS.

83

USERNAME: BWAYNE
RE: JOURNAL ENTRY 6

THE KRYPTONIAN MUSEUM WE FOUND FOR SHELTER FROM THE
SANDSTORMS EXPLAINED A LOT. WE'RE STUCK HERE IN THIS
PHANTOM DETENTION.

LUTHORCORP MUST'VE RECOVERED THE PROJECTOR TECHNOLOGY
AS PART OF THE SPACE DEBRIS THEY COLLECTED IN
SMALLVILLE FOLLOWING THE METEOR SHOWER. AND ONCE LEX
FOUND OUT WHAT HIS FATHER HAD, HE FOUND A WAY TO
INSTALL THIS PHANTOM DETENTION PROJECTOR INTO CLARK'S
TROPHY TO SEND HIM AND THE REST OF US HERE.

I'M GOING TO GET OUT OF HERE, AND WHEN I DO, I'M
GOING TO TAKE LEX LUTHOR DOWN! AND I'LL HAVE HELP. WE
DISCOVERED SOME ITEMS IN THE SAND THAT LED US TO OTHER
KIDS TRAPPED HERE. I JUST NEVER THOUGHT IT WOULD BE
THEM . . .

ITEMS FOUND IN SAND

TEETH

JOKER FISH

CLOWN YOYO

FLOWER PRANK

86

USERNAME: BWAYNE
RE: JOURNAL ENTRY 7

IT APPEARS CLARK WAS RIGHT. WE'RE NOT THE ONLY ONES
STUCK HERE. BUT THE JOKER AND HARLEY AREN'T WELCOME
COMPANY. HOW CAN I FORGET ALL THE TIMES THEY PULLED
PRANKS ON ME AT SCHOOL? PULLING OUT MY CHAIR. THROWING
PIES AT ME. THE FOOD FIGHTS IN THE CAFETERIA.

EVERY TIME THEY'RE AROUND, THEY'RE NOTHING BUT
TROUBLE. BUT CLARK FEELS SORRY FOR THEM AND WANTS TO
GIVE THEM A CHANCE. PLUS, WE CAN USE ALL THE HELP WE
CAN GET TRYING TO FIND A WAY OUT.

SINCE I CONSIDER THEM MORE LIKE SUSPECTS THAN
FRIENDS, MAYBE IT'S TIME TO PUT MY DETECTIVE SKILLS
TO USE. TRY TO FIND OUT WHAT THEY KNOW AND IF IT'S
ANY HELP TO US . . .

GCPD JUNIOR DETECTIV
INTERROGATION NOTES

SUBJECTS: THE JOKER AND HARLEY
CRIME: WRONG PLACE, WRONG TIME
SUSPECTS: UNDETERMINED

THE JOKER AND HARLEY WERE FOUND INSIDE THE
PHANTOM DETENTION, CLAIMING TO BE PRISONERS.
THEIR EXCUSE WAS THAT LEX WANTED TO RECRUIT
THEM INTO HIS LITTLE BAD GUY GANG, BUT THEY
DIDN'T WANT TO HAVE ANYTHING TO DO WITH IT.
THE JOKER FOUND THE WHOLE THING TO BE A LAUGH
RIOT. HARLEY FELT ALLERGIC TO CATS, EVEN
THOUGH CHEETAH JUST WEARS A CATSUIT.

LEX DIDN'T CARE FOR THEIR REASONS AND
TOOK OFFENSE. SO HE OPENED UP THE PHANTOM
DETENTION AND KEPT THEM PRISONER HERE. ONCE
HE KNEW IT WORKED, HE USED THE TECHNOLOGY TO
PLAN HIS CAPTURE OF CLARK AND THE REST OF US.

THEY ALSO DON'T KNOW HOW TO GET OUT OF THE
PHANTOM DETENTION.

HARD TO KNOW IF THEY'RE TELLING THE TRUTH.
THEY'VE ALWAYS BEEN OBNOXIOUS AND CLASS
CLOWNS. BUT I'LL GO ALONG WITH IT FOR NOW.

ONE OF THE THINGS I'VE NOTICED IS THAT TIME HAS NO
MEANING IN PHANTOM DETENTION. THE SUN DOESN'T SET.
IT FEELS LIKE WE'VE BEEN WALKING FOR DAYS OR WEEKS,
MAYBE EVEN LONGER. OR IT COULD BE ONLY MINUTES THAT
ARE STRETCHED OUT. IT'S HARD TO KNOW FOR SURE, SINCE
THERE ARE BROKEN CLOCKS EVERYWHERE.

FOR NOW, THE JOKER AND HARLEY ARE PART OF OUR GROUP.
I THINK THEY'RE MORE TROUBLE THAN THEY'RE WORTH,
ALWAYS JOKING AND PRANKING AND LAUGHING. BUT I
REALIZE THEY'RE STUCK IN HERE JUST LIKE WE ARE. AND
IF WE CAN ALL FIND THE EXIT AND GET OUT TOGETHER,
THEN THAT'S A WORTHY GOAL.

JUST NO MORE PIES OR SAND IN MY FACE!

94

95

USERNAME: BWAYNE
RE: JOURNAL ENTRY 9

THIS PHANTOM DETENTION IS REALLY DANGEROUS! EVERY
SHADOW HAS THE POSSIBILITY OF A PHANTOM HIDING IN
IT. WHEN WE WEREN'T PAYING ATTENTION, THE PHANTOMS
APPEARED AND KIDNAPPED BARRY AND THE JOKER. WITH-
OUT THOSE TWO AROUND TO CONSTANTLY TALK, JOKE, AND
ANNOY, IT'S A LOT MORE QUIET. IN A WAY, I KIND OF
LIKE IT. BUT IT'S NO REASON FOR THEM TO BE TAKEN.

WE NEED TO FIND BOTH OF THEM AND GET THEM BACK AND
THEN FIND A WAY OUT OF HERE. WE'VE BEEN HERE LONG
ENOUGH. AND THE LONGER WE'RE STUCK HERE, THE WORSE
IT GETS.

PLUS, I'VE GOT A CAVE I STILL NEED TO FIX UP.

99

102

SCAN AREA INDETERMINATE
TARGET LOCATIONS UNKNOWN

UNKNOWN VIRUS DETECTED

    HACK LOCATION—PROCESSING . . .

WELCOMMME TO THE PHANTOMMM DETENTION ZONE
WE ARE ALLLL PHANTOMMMS HERE
LET US TOUCH YOUUU
TO TURNNN YOU INNNTO GHOSTS
TO JOIN THE OTHERSSS

USERNAME: BWAYNE
RE: JOURNAL ENTRY 10

I'M WRITING THIS IN DARKNESS WITH ONLY THE DRONE SCREEN
LIGHT TO HELP ME SEE. THIS LIGHT MIGHT COME IN HANDY
FOR MORE THAN JUST WRITING, SO I'M GOING TO WRITE DOWN
AS MUCH AS I CAN TO KEEP IT ON.

WE ENTERED THE SHADOWLANDS IN SEARCH OF OUR MISSING
FRIENDS AND TOOK PRECAUTIONS TO STAY TOGETHER. BUT ONE
AFTER THE OTHER STARTED TO DISAPPEAR. AND NOW I'M THE
LAST ONE AND ALL ALONE.

BY MYSELF, IN THE DARK . . . YOU WOULD THINK I'D LIKE
THIS. NORMALLY I'D AGREE, BUT NOT THIS TIME. I NEED MY
FRIENDS. AND I WILL FIND THEM ALL, EVEN IF I HAVE TO DO
IT BY MYSELF.

WHEN THESE PHANTOMS TOUCH ANYONE, THEY TAKE THEIR
BODIES TO "TIME-OUT" WHILE THEIR GHOSTS WANDER AND
REMAIN LOST. BUT I'M ALWAYS PREPARED FOR ANYTHING.
I THINK I CAN USE MY COMPUTER TO HELP FIND EVERYONE
AND GET THEM BACK TO NORMAL SO WE CAN GET OUT OF THIS
DETENTION. AT LEAST I THINK I CAN. I'VE NEVER ACTUALLY
DONE THIS BEFORE, SO WISH ME LUCK!

ALFRED WOULD LAUGH EVERY TIME I LOCKED MYSELF IN THE
CLOSET OR HID UNDER THE BED. OR THOSE TIMES I WOULD GO
DOWN INTO THE BATCAVE AT NIGHT WITHOUT A FLASHLIGHT.
I'D USE THE EXCUSE THAT I WAS SLEEPWALKING, WHEN REALLY
I WAS JUST TRAINING MYSELF TO SEE BETTER IN THE DARK.
NOW ALL THAT TRAINING IS ABOUT TO PAY OFF.

THESE PHANTOMS LIKE THE DARKNESS, BUT SO DO I. AND
THERE'S NO WAY I'M GETTING STUCK IN DETENTION WITHOUT
RESCUING MY FRIENDS.

THESE PHANTOMS PICKED THE WRONG KID TO PICK ON!
I'M GOING TO RUN A SONAR GHOST LOCATING PROGRAM ON MY
DRONE. THEY WON'T SEE THIS COMING . . .

111

113

I'VE SEEN A LOT OF CRAZY THINGS. VILLAINS. EVIL ROBOTS. ALIENS. MONSTERS. BUT I NEVER THOUGHT I'D SEE GHOSTS. ALFRED WOULD SAY I LIVE A CHARMED LIFE. AND I WOULD TELL ALFRED . . . YES, NOW CAN WE PLEASE ORDER PIZZA?

I WAS LUCKY TO BE ABLE TO FIND ALL MY FRIENDS. ONCE I DEFEATED THE PHANTOMS, EVERYONE TURNED BACK TO THEIR NORMAL SELVES. IT WAS WEIRD.

NOW THAT WE'RE OUT OF THE SHADOWLANDS, IT'S TIME TO FIX MY DRONE. WITHOUT A WORKING HOMING BEACON, WE'D BE STUCK HERE FOREVER. AND IT'S PAST TIME WE GOT OUT OF HERE!

TRACKING SUSPECTS

EVERYONE LEAVES TRACKS WHEREVER THEY GO. THESE ARE SOME HELPFUL THINGS TO KEEP IN MIND WHILE TRACKING YOUR SUSPECT:

- KNOW THE TRACKS OF THE PERSON YOU'RE TRYING TO FIND
- ELIMINATE OTHER TRACKS TO NARROW YOUR SEARCH
- DON'T EXPECT TO FIND PERFECT TRACKS
- LOOK FOR HEEL MARKS
- THE TOE WILL NOT LEAVE A HEAVY PRINT
- PEOPLE PUT THEIR FEET UP WHEN THEY RELAX, SO LOOK AROUND
- MARKS CAN BE LEFT WHEN CLIMBING OVER OBSTRUCTIONS
- PEOPLE DIG IN THEIR TOES MORE WHEN WALKING ON AN INCLINE
- PATTERNS CAN TRANSFER FROM ONE SURFACE TO ANOTHER

119

- THE SPACES BETWEEN FOOTPRINTS ARE LONGER FOR RUNNING, SHORTER FOR WALKING
- DON'T GET FOOLED IF TRACKS CROSS ONE ANOTHER
- LOOK AROUND FOR ANYTHING INTERRUPTED
- CLUES ARE EVERYWHERE

KNOCK KNOCK!
WHO'S THERE?
"LOST"
"LOST" WHO?
LOST ALL OF YOU!
HEE HEE HEEEEEE

131

"BATMAN'S GUIDE TO BEATING BATMAN"
BY BATMAN, FOR BATMAN

NO ONE CAN BEAT BATMAN . . . EXCEPT FOR BATMAN.
SO TO BEAT BATMAN, YOU MUST BE BATMAN!
THESE ARE SOME TIPS FOR WHAT TO DO:

1) FIRST YOU MUST BE BATMAN. ALWAYS BE BATMAN.

2) BATMAN KNOWS HOW TO BEAT EVERYONE. KNOW EVERYTHING HE KNOWS.

3) PULL HIS EARS.

4) PULL HIS CAPE.

5) PULL HIS LEG (JOKES HELP, BAD JOKES HELP BETTER).

6) WHEN ALL ELSE FAILS . . . FIGHT DIRTY. BECAUSE HE WON'T.

135

137

139

142

USERNAME: BWAYNE
RE: JOURNAL ENTRY 12

I'M TYPING THIS ON MY RECOVERED BATCOMPUTER. EVEN THOUGH THE JOKER AND HARLEY STOLE IT AND THE DRONE, WE WERE ABLE TO GET IT BACK. THEY'VE RUN OFF AGAIN, PRESUMABLY TO CAUSE MORE TROUBLE.

ALSO, THE DRONE IS FIXED, MEANING WE'VE BEEN ABLE TO LOCATE THE BEACON. WE CAN GO BACK TO THE ENTRANCE AND TRY TO FIND OUR WAY HOME. WE'RE ONE STEP CLOSER TO GETTING OUT OF HERE! I'M NOT LOOKING FORWARD TO RETURNING TO HOMEWORK AND AWARDS CEREMONIES. BUT I AM LOOKING FORWARD TO GETTING SAND OUT OF MY SHOES.

147

148

ALFRED'S "TO DO" LIST

- shop for groceries
                        PICK UP PUDDING CUPS —B
- make beds and fold sheets

- wash laundry

- fix leaky sink in guest bathroom #7

- prune trees in garden and water plants

- car maintenance (wax limo, check tires, change
  oil, clean garage)

- prepare school lunches for next week

- clean Master Bruce's other room at precisely
  4:00 PM

- create weekend dinner menu

153

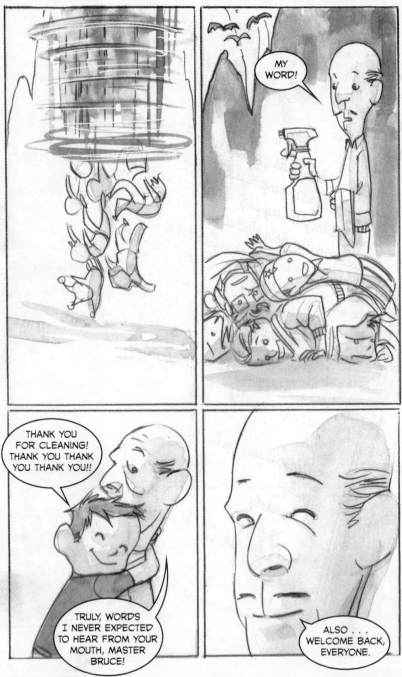

Master Bruce,

I hope this letter finds you safe upon your return. It has been hard to keep myself busy without you around to brighten my day. No kitchen accidents to clean up. No dirty clothes to pick up after. No healthy meals to make or vegetables to force you to eat. No science experiments gone wrong or fire departments to call. Even the bats are staying quiet in the cave and not getting into the house.

Yes, without you around, things are much more quiet and peaceful.

Please return soon!!

Sincerely,

Alfred

USERNAME: BWAYNE
RE: JOURNAL ENTRY 13

WE'RE HOME!!!

I WAS SUCCESSFUL IN REMEMBERING ALFRED'S CLEANING
SCHEDULE. HIS HELP ACTIVATING THE DOORWAY INTO
THE PHANTOM DETENTION ZONE ALLOWED US TO ESCAPE.
NOT ALL OF US WERE SO LUCKY. BIZARRO WAS LEFT
BEHIND. BUT IF HE HADN'T BEEN, THEN DOOMSDAY
MIGHT'VE GOTTEN FREE TO STOP US. IT WAS A NOBLE
SACRIFICE BY A REAL HERO.

NOW THAT WE'RE BACK, WE HAVE NO TIME TO REST.
OUR SIGHTS ARE SET BACK ON LEX. HE'S THE ONE
RESPONSIBLE FOR ALL OUR PROBLEMS. AND HE'S THE
ONE WE NEED TO BRING TO JUSTICE!

BUT FIRST, SOMETHING TO EAT. ALFRED IS ALREADY
IN THE KITCHEN PREPARING OUR MEAL. HE GUARANTEES
ME IT'S NOT PIZZA, BUT MY DETECTIVE SENSE SMELLS
PEPPERONI.

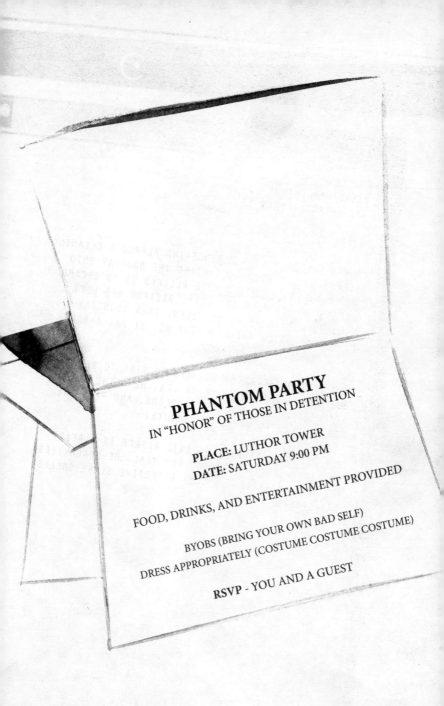

PHANTOM PARTY
IN "HONOR" OF THOSE IN DETENTION

PLACE: LUTHOR TOWER
DATE: SATURDAY 9:00 PM

FOOD, DRINKS, AND ENTERTAINMENT PROVIDED

BYOBS (BRING YOUR OWN BAD SELF)
DRESS APPROPRIATELY (COSTUME COSTUME COSTUME)

RSVP - YOU AND A GUEST

MAP OF LUTHOR TOWER ELEVATOR SHAFTS

thanks Ollie for snagging that invite

it's the perfect plan

happy to help stick it to Lex

we get inside, avoid detection, and drop off the package

hows everyone doing? check in

Here

inside but hiding in a room

I'm stuck in one of the elevators

I touched all the floor buttons out of habit

can you help us out Vic?

of course

let me see what I can do

SEND

ELEVATOR
FIRE ALARM

hack went smooth

was able to provide all of you some cover or help

security cameras are on a loop and some shut down

rooms you need are unlocked

thanks Vic

you found all the alarms and shut them off?

pretty sure I spotted all of them

I'll check again

SEND

PARTY PHOTOS

163

ALFRED,

IF YOU'RE READING THIS, IT'S BECAUSE THINGS WENT BAD AND I WAS CAUGHT. MY DAYS OF DETECTIVE CRIME FIGHTING ARE OVER AND EVIL HAS WON . . . BUT NOT FOR LONG.

WITH MY HELPFUL ADVICE, YOU CAN AVENGE ME AND DEFEAT EVIL. FOLLOW MY INSTRUCTIONS:

1) BECOME A SUPER HERO (YOU DON'T NEED POWERS FOR THIS . . . TRUST ME).

2) TRAIN HARD. I REALIZE YOU'RE OLD, BUT THAT'S NO EXCUSE. THERE'S ALWAYS GADGETS AND ROBOTS TO HELP YOU. USE MY ALLOWANCE TO BUY THEM.

3) THERE IS TONS OF USEFUL INFORMATION TO HELP YOU ON MY COMPUTER. TO ACCESS IT, MY PASSCODE IS BAT1234. IF I'M NOT CAUGHT, DON'T USE MY PASSWORD TO SNOOP. I WILL CHANGE IT WHEN I GET BACK!

4) GET RID OF THE LIMO. GET A BETTER CAR TO FIGHT CRIME IN. SOMETHING SPORTY.

5) MAKE SURE TO IRON YOUR CAPE. IT WRINKLES EASY.

YOU ARE VENGEANCE. YOU ARE THE NIGHT. YOU ARE . . . BAT-ALFRED.

-BRUCE

TO ALFRED
IN CASE OF EMERGENCY

168

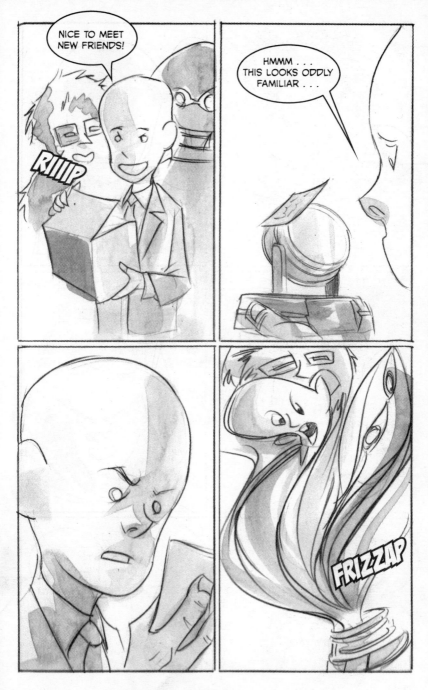

169

LEX,

IF YOU'RE READING THIS, THEN YOU'RE BEING PUNISHED FOR YOUR ACTIONS BY BEING SENT TO PHANTOM DETENTION. DON'T WORRY. WE'LL LET YOU OUT ... EVENTUALLY. BUT WHILE YOU'RE IN THERE, YOU WON'T BE ALONE.

— BRUCE, CLARK, DIANA, OLLIE, BARRY

USERNAME: BWAYNE
RE: JOURNAL ENTRY 14

LEX AND HIS BULLY FRIENDS HAVE BEEN SENT TO
DETENTION . . . PHANTOM DETENTION! IT WAS
SO GREAT TO TURN THE TABLES ON LEX AFTER
EVERYTHING HE PUT US THROUGH. I'D LOVE TO SEE
THE LOOK ON HIS FACE WHEN HE REALIZES WE'RE
THE ONES RESPONSIBLE. COULDN'T HAVE HAPPENED
TO A WORSE GUY.

IT'S SO GOOD TO BE HOME. I HOPE I NEVER HAVE
TO GO TO ANOTHER AWARDS CEREMONY FOR THE REST
OF MY LIFE. IN FACT, I'D LIKE TO JUST CHANGE
MY STUDIES. MAYBE I CAN ENCOURAGE ALFRED TO
GET ME A PRIVATE TUTOR. MAYBE I CAN TRAVEL
AROUND THE WORLD AND LEARN FROM THE BEST
TEACHERS IN EVERY FIELD.

AFTER THE CRAZY ADVENTURE WE JUST HAD, WE'RE
ALL EXCITED TO BE HONORING OUR OWN PERSONAL
HEROES IN OUR LIVES . . .

Diana at home

Barry in school

Derek Fridolfs

Derek Fridolfs is a *New York Times* bestselling writer. With Dustin Nguyen, he cowrote the Eisner-nominated *Batman: Li'l Gotham*. He's also worked on a range of titles including *Arkham City* with Paul Dini, *Adventures of Superman*, *Detective Comics*, *Sensation Comics Featuring Wonder Woman*, and comics based on Grumpy Cat and WWE pro wrestling. He's written and drawn comics based on the cartoons *Adventure Time*, *Regular Show*, *Clarence*, *Pig Goat Banana Cricket*, *Pink Panther's The Inspector*, *Dexter's Laboratory*, *Teenage Mutant Ninja Turtles*, *Teen Titans Go!*, *Looney Tunes*, and *Scooby-Doo, Where Are You!* Recently, Derek has also been fortunate to collaborate with producer/screenwriter Bob Gale to cowrite a *Back to the Future* miniseries called *Biff to the Future*.

Dustin Nguyen

Dustin Nguyen is a *New York Times* bestselling and Eisner Award–winning American comics creator. His body of work includes the co-creation of *Batman: Li'l Gotham*, numerous DC, Marvel, Dark Horse, and Boom! titles along with Image Comics' *Descender*, which he co-created. He lives in California with his wife, Nicole; their two kids, Bradley and Kaeli; and dog, Max. His first children's picture book, titled *What Is It?*, is written by his wife (at the age of 10) and is their first collaboration together. He enjoys sleeping and driving.